D1177540

Bill Martin Jr and
Michael Sampson

Illustrated by Nathalie Beauvois

Bing! Bang! Chugga! Beep!

Brown Books Kids
Dallas / New York
www.BrownBooksKids.com
(972) 381-0009

A New Era in Publishing®

Distributed in New Zealand and Australia by David Bateman Ltd.

Publisher's Cataloging-In-Publication Data

Names: Martin, Bill, 1916-2004, author. | Sampson, Michael R., author. | Beauvois, Nathalie (Illustrator), illustrator.
Title: Bing! Bang! Chugga! Beep! / Bill Martin Jr and Michael Sampson ; illustrated by Nathalie Beauvois.
Description: Dallas ; New York : Brown Books Kids, [2023] | Interest age level: 004-008. | Summary: Bing! Bang! Chugga! Beep! is the latest charming tale from rhyming pair Bill Martin Jr and Michael Sampson. This old car has been everywhere from the backyard to the sky, from the hills to the water. Bouncing between the mud in the ground and the clouds up high, the old car is loved by a clever young boy ... --Publisher.
Identifiers: ISBN: 9781612545998 (hardcover)
Subjects: LCSH: Antique and classic cars--Juvenile fiction. | Boys--Juvenile fiction. | Locomotion-- Juvenile fiction. | Mud--Juvenile fiction. | CYAC: Antique and classic cars--Fiction. | Boys-- Fiction. | Locomotion--Fiction. | Mud--Fiction. | LCGFT: Stories in rhyme. | BISAC: JUVENILE FICTION / Stories in Verse. | JUVENILE FICTION / Transportation / Cars & Trucks.
Classification: LCC: PZ8.3.M418 B56 2023 | DDC: [E]--dc23

This book has been officially leveled by using the F&P Text Level Gradient™ Leveling System.

ISBN 978-1-61254-599-8
LCCN 2022948889

Printed in China
10 9 8 7 6 5 4 3 2 1

For more information or to contact the author, please go to www.MichaelSampson.com.

MS—To Rhett, Reid, and Rowan

NB—To Marce and his love for cars

This old car,

it is blue,

Yellow, red, and purple too,

With a bing, bang,

Chugga, beep,

Bouncing here and there,

This old car goes everywhere.

This old car,
it goes beep,
Wakes the neighbors
from their sleep,
With a bing,
bang,
Chugga,
beep,

**Bouncing here
and there,
This old car goes
everywhere.**

This old car, climbs the hill,
To the top like Jack and Jill,
With a
bing,
bang

Bouncing here
and there,
This old car
goes everywhere.

This old car, it does tricks,
Jumping over ten red bricks,
With a

bing, bang,
Chugga, beep,

Bouncing here
and there,
This old car
goes everywhere.

This old car, it can fly,
Soaring high into the sky,

With a

bing,

bang,

Chugga,

beep,

Bouncing here and there,
This old car goes
everywhere.

This old car, it can race,
Driving fast to
win first place,
With a

bing,
bang,
Chugga,
beep,

Bouncing here and there,
This old car goes everywhere.

This old car, it's my buddy,
Even when it's wet and muddy,
With a **bing, bang,
Chugga, beep,**
Bouncing here and there,
This old car goes everywhere.

Charlie, it's time to come in for your bath.

This old car, it can hide,
When it's time to go inside,
With a

bing, bang,
Chugga, beep,

Bouncing here
and there,
This old car goes
everywhere.

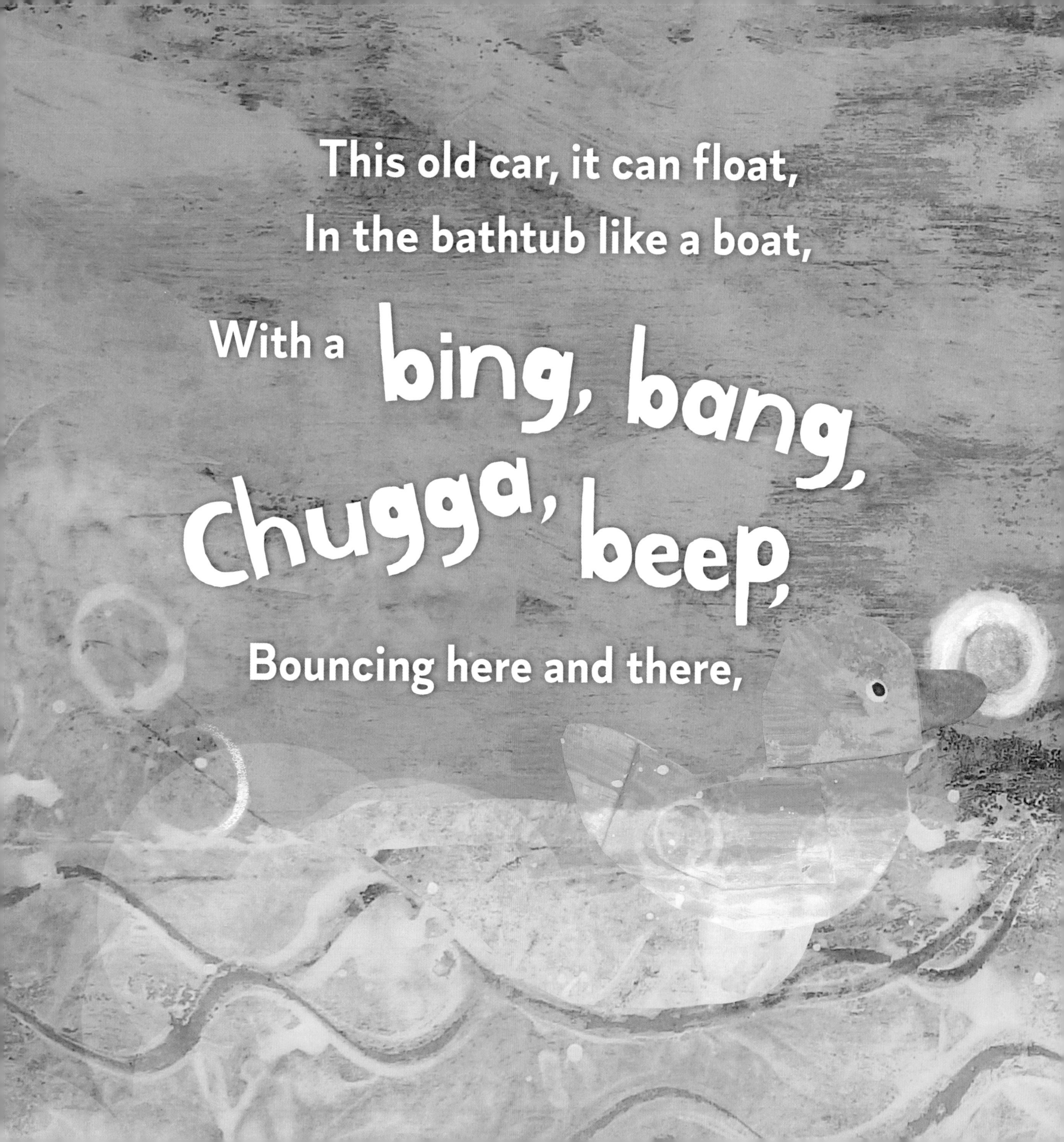

This old car, it can float,
In the bathtub like a boat,

With a **bing, bang,**
Chugga, beep,

Bouncing here and there,

This old car
goes everywhere.

This old car, it's my toy,
Driving it is such a joy,
With a **bing,**
bang,
Chugga,
beep,
Off we go to bed.

"Have sweet dreams,"
my mother said.

What's your favorite toy car to play with?
Tractor
Station Wagon
Dump Truck
Fire Truck
Classic Car
Race Car
Police Car
Van
Sports Car